Foxwood Tales

presents the story of
Harvey
Rue and Willy in....

For Sarah, Nicholas and Andrew

First U.S. edition 1985
by Barron's Educational Series, Inc.

First published in 1985 by
André Deutsch Limited
105 Great Russell Street, London WC1

All inquiries should be addressed to:
Barron's Educational Series, Inc.
113 Crossways Park Drive
Woodbury, New York 11797

International Standard Book No. 0–8120–5664–7

Library of Congress Catalog no. 85–1407
Printed in Spain
5678   987654321

The Foxwood Treasure

Written and Illustrated by
Cynthia & Brian Paterson

BARRON'S
Woodbury, New York • London • Toronto • Sydney

The thick red jam bubbling in the old black pot had made the kitchen hot and steamy.

Mrs. Hedgehog turned to her son, Willy, who was sitting at the kitchen table staring at nothing in particular.

"What's the matter with you?" she asked irritably.

"I'm bored," he said. "There's never anything to do here."

"Never anything to do," she said indignantly. "I've got a million and one things to do, so you can help me out."

Willy groaned. "That's not what I meant," he said.

Mrs. Hedgehog took no notice. "You can take this basket of fruit and pickles and go and visit Grandpa," she went on. "That will keep you out of mischief and out of my way. Make sure you go and give him my love."

Off Willy trotted with the basket. He hadn't gone far when he met Harvey Mouse and Rue Rabbit.

"I've got to take these things to Grandpa's," he told them, "so I can't play."

"We've got nothing to do," said Rue. "Can we come with you?"

"If you'll take turns to carry the basket," answered Willy. "It's heavy and I need a rest."

They found Grandpa busy painting his old bicycle.

"Mom's sent over some pickles, Grandpa," shouted Willy.

"Oh, just the job, young Willy," replied Grandpa. Harvey and Rue were looking at the bicycle.

"Can we help you paint?" asked Harvey.

"No thanks," said Grandpa, "I've just finished it. I'm going to the meeting at Mrs. Mole's house now. Would you like to come along?"

A meeting didn't sound very interesting, but as there was nothing else to do they decided to go with him.

A big crowd had squeezed into Mrs. Mole's front room for the meeting.

"What's it about, Grandpa?" whispered Willy.

"We need a village hall," he answered, "but funds are low, so we want everyone to think of ways of raising money."

"Silence please," shouted Mr. Gruffey, the badger, banging a wooden mallet on Mrs. Mole's best polished table.

"Oh dear," she murmured, "the sooner we get a village hall the better."

The meeting went on a long time, and by the time it had ended Harvey, Rue and Willy were wishing they hadn't come. But they did like the idea of raising money, and afterward Willy asked his grandfather what they could do to help.

"Why don't we go along to the library," said Grandpa thoughtfully, "to find out how the famous animals of Foxwood made money in the past. There are a couple of old books I would like you to read. They might give you some ideas."

"Old books," said Willy in disgust. "You can't raise money by reading old books. We want to *do* something!"

Grandpa didn't seem to hear Willy's grumble. He just gave him the names of two books and told him to ask Mrs. Squirrel for them. Then he went off to arrange the next meeting with Mr. Gruffey and Mrs. Mole while the three friends settled themselves in a quiet corner of the library.

After a while Mrs. Squirrel appeared with two large books, which she placed on the table in front of them. Rue took one and opened it.

"What have you got?" asked Willy, peering over Rue's shoulder. "History," said Rue. "It's all about the famous animals who used to live in the village – Captain Weasel and Lord and Lady Moleworthy. They were very rich and lived in a mansion called Foxwood Park. Oh, here's a bit about Squire Fox . . ."

"I know all about him," interrupted Willy. "Grandpa told me. That's his statue in the village square."

"Everyone knows that, smarty," said Rue. "What else do you know?"

"That's it, really," said Willy, feeling rather squashed. He wished he'd listened more carefully when Grandpa was telling him about Foxwood in the old days.

"It says here," read Rue, "that he was a jolly chap and everyone liked him. He owned a magnificent den hidden somewhere near Foxwood, and he used to invite his friends there for an evening's merrymaking, but he would always meet them at the edge of the wood and blindfold them before leading them to his den."

"Why, didn't he trust them?" interrupted Harvey.

"It doesn't say," Rue went on, "but apparently one dreadful night he was followed home by a gang of thieves. There was a terrific fight and he was robbed of almost everything."

"He left his ruined den and built an inn called The Old Fox where he served a special lemonade made from his own secret recipe. When he died the inn was shut up, and the recipe has never been found."

"That's right," interrupted Willy. "Grandpa told me where the inn was."

"If he hid the secret recipe in the inn and if we could find it, we could make a fortune," said Harvey.

"Your grandpa was right," said Rue. "The old books have given us an idea."

"Let's start looking first thing tomorrow morning," said Willy.

The next morning they met at Squire Fox's statue and headed into the woods. After searching for nearly an hour, they found an overgrown path and followed it, pushing through brambles, grasses and bushes till suddenly they found themselves standing in front of a crumbling old house with an inn sign swinging crookedly from a pole above the door.

"This is it," shouted Rue, "we've found it. Give the door a good push."

They did, and slowly it creaked open.

Dust and cobwebs covered everything inside, and at the far end of
the room stood a bar. Willy ran behind it and pulled a pump handle.

"What'll it be, gentlemen?" he asked.

"Two glasses of lemonade special, please," replied Harvey.

"That'll be 25 cents," said Willy, pretending to ring up the till.

"I'll be Squire Fox," said Rue. "Would you gentlemen like rooms
for the night? You would? Then come this way, and watch your heads."

He led the way to the stairs, followed by Harvey. Willy stayed
where he was, for the stairs looked rotten, and they were dark.

"I think I'll wait for you down here," he said.

As soon as the others had disappeared, Willy wished he had gone with them. The bar was eerie, and he jumped when a board creaked.

"Who's there?" he called.

"Only me," answered a squeaky little voice, and to Willy's surprise out popped a mouse from behind the grandfather clock in the corner.

"I'm Barty," he said cheerfully, "I live here and keep the place clean. Who are you?"

"I'm Willy, and I've come to look for Squire Fox's secret recipe."

"I can show you lots of secret places," said Barty, "but I'm blessed if I know what a recipe is."

Willy wasn't too sure what a recipe would look like either. "I think it would be hidden in a secret place," he said hopefully.

"Come on, then," said Barty, and joining Willy behind the bar, he pulled a pump handle marked *Special*. Suddenly a tiny door opened in the biggest barrel.

"Squeeze in," said Barty, "it's quite safe." Willy stepped inside, and the door slammed shut behind them.

Harvey and Rue were nosing about upstairs when they heard a door slam.

"I think we'd better see if Willy's all right," said Harvey. They ran down the stairs.

"Willy," called Rue, as they reached the bar.

No reply.

"Come on, we've got something to show you," he coaxed, thinking Willy was probably hiding for a joke.

Still no reply.

"Where on earth can he have gone?" asked Harvey. "We've only been gone a few minutes."

"I bet he's gone home," said Rue. "That door banging probably frightened him."

"If he has, he can stay there tomorrow," said Harvey crossly. "Anyway it's late, so we'd better go. We'll speak to Willy in the morning."

The next morning Harvey and Rue knocked loudly on Mrs. Hedgehog's door.

"Where's Willy?" Rue asked her. "We've got a bone to pick with him."

"Not here you haven't," replied Willy's mother, "because he didn't come home last night. He told me he would stay with his grandfather, and that's where you'll find him now."

Rue and Harvey were becoming more and more cross with Willy for wasting so much time, and when they reached Grandpa's cottage they knocked even louder on the door.

"Go away," groaned Grandpa. "It's too early to wake people."

"Tell Willy we want him," said Harvey. "Then we'll go away."

"I can't do that," said Grandpa firmly, "because he's not here." And he slammed the door.

"Not here and not at home," said Harvey in dismay. "Then . . . oh . . . no. The old inn. He must still be there. Quick!"

They ran all the way back to the inn and searched it from top to bottom. There was no sign of Willy. "If he doesn't show up soon," said Harvey as they walked back to the village, "we'll have to tell his mother."

There was a bench at the foot of Squire Fox's statue, and Harvey and Rue sat down on it, too tired and worried to talk about what to do next. Suddenly the statue spoke.

"Is anyone there?" it asked. Harvey and Rue jumped up, terrified. Strange scratching noises came from inside the statue.

"It's haunted," cried Harvey.

"No it's not," said the statue. "It's me. I can't get out."

"That's Willy's voice," shouted Rue happily. "He's in the statue."

Then, to their amazement, they heard another voice. "There's a door here," it said. "If we push can you pull?"

Harvey and Rue prodded frantically around the base of the statue. Suddenly Rue felt a movement. "Got it," he called. "Push as hard as you can."

A stone panel opened an inch. Harvey grabbed the edge, Rue grabbed Harvey and together they tugged.

The stone flew open and Willy tumbled out onto the ground, followed by Barty.

"Where on earth have you been?" asked Harvey. "We were just going to organize a search party, and who's that . . . ?"

"It's Barty," answered Willy, "and we've found Squire Fox's den. Come on. We'll show you."

As Harvey and Rue crawled along the narrow passage, they thought Willy must be braver than he seemed, for it was cold and damp and very dark. Suddenly, however, the passage opened out into a beautiful, high-ceilinged hall. They stared in wonder. At last Rue spoke.

"To think it's been here in the village all this time," he said, "and no one knew. Cunning old fox. Fox Hall!"

"Fox Hall!" echoed Harvey. "The hall! That's it. The village hall. Willy, you and Barty have found the new village hall!"

"That's not all we've found," said Willy. "Look at this. It's the secret lemonade recipe. Barty lined a secret drawer in this old chest with it; he didn't know it was valuable."

"Hooray!" said Harvey. "Now that you've found the recipe, we can make the lemonade again. We'll make it famous and we'll be famous, too."

"Not just us," said Willy thoughtfully. "It was Grandpa who gave us the book about Squire Fox."

The whole village celebrated the news that Willy and his new friend, Barty, had found Fox Hall, and at the last meeting at Mrs. Mole's house they decided to reopen the Old Fox Inn with a grand party.

Grandpa made a barrel of special lemonade, and animals came from far and wide just to taste the delicious brew. The party was a huge success and raised more than enough money to build a new entrance to Fox Hall.

Grandpa enjoyed the gala opening of the Old Fox Inn so much that he stayed on and became the best landlord the village had had since Squire Fox himself.

Willy and Barty were given the honor of cutting the ribbon at the opening of the new village hall, and Barty stayed on as caretaker. Harvey and Rue weren't forgotten, either, for together with Willy and Barty they got the best reward of all. As much lemonade as they could wish for. Free forever.

The End